STEPHEN GAMMELL
ONCE upon MacDONALD'S FARM

Simon & Schuster Books for Young Readers

Simon & Schuster Books for Young Readers
An imprint of Simon & Schuster Children's Publishing Division
1230 Avenue of the Americas, New York, New York 10020

1   3   5   7   9   10   8   6   4   2

Library of Congress Cataloging-in-Publication Data
Gammell, Stephen.
Once upon MacDonald's farm / Stephen Gammell.—Rev. format ed.
p.   cm.
Summary : MacDonald tries farming with exotic circus animals,
but has better luck with his neighbor's cow, horse, and chicken—or does he?
ISBN 0-689-82885-3
[1. Farm life Fiction. 2. Animals Fiction. 3. Humorous stories.] I. Title.
PZ7.G144On 2000   [E]—dc21   99-30691   CIP

TO MY DEAR ONE,
MY FAMILY,
AND
SULLY

"I REALLY **MUST** HAVE SOME ANIMALS."

He ALSo BOUGHT a BABOON and A LiON.

IN the MORNING, MacDONALD AND THE ELEPHANT WENT OUT to THE FiELD...

to DO THE PLOWING.

MUCH LatER thAT AFTERNOON,

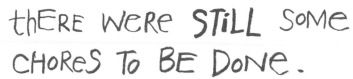

tHERE WERE **STILL** SoME CHoReS To BE DoNe.

BUT WHILE HE WAS SLEEPING,
THE ANIMALS DECIDED TO LEAVE.
AND SO THEY DID.

WITHOUT
a SOUND.

THAT EVENING, HE SENT OVER a HORSE, a COW, and a CHICKEN.

BUT FIRST THE PLOWING.

The illustrations in this book were created in 1981 and reseparated for this edition.
They are rendered in pencil.

Hand-lettering by Stephen Gammell

Book design by Heather Wood and Stephen Gammell

The paper is 140 GSM Japan Silver Ring Glazed Woodfree stock

Both text and jacket are printed by South China Printing Company, Hong Kong